Cherokee Bat and the Goat
Guys
Francesca Lia Block
AR B.L.: 5.0
Points: 3.0

Also by Francesca Lia Block

cherokee bat

and the goat guys

FRANCESCA LIA BLOCK

A Charlotte Zolotow Book

HarperTrophy®
An Imprint of HarperCollinsPublishers

With deep thanks to my editors,
Charlotte Zolotow and Joanna Cotler

"Song of Encouragement" (Papago), from *Singing for Power: The Song Magic of the Papago Indians of Southern Arizona* by Ruth Underhill. Copyright © 1938, 1966 by Ruth Murray Underhill. Reprinted by permission of the University of California Press.

"Wind Song" (Pima), "Song of Fallen Deer" (Pima), "Omen" (Aztec), and "Dream Song" (Wintu) are excerpts from *In the Trail of the Wind* edited by John Bierhorst. Copyright © 1971 by John Bierhorst. Reprinted by permission of Farrar, Straus and Giroux, Inc.

Cherokee Bat and the Goat Guys
Copyright © 1992 by Francesca Lia Block

Library of Congress Cataloging-in-Publication Data
Block, Francesca Lia.
    Cherokee Bat and the Goat Guys / Francesca Lia Block
        p.   cm.
    "A Charlotte Zolotow book."
    Summary: With their parents away, four young people form a rock band that becomes wildly popular, carrying them into a "freer" life than they can cope with.
    ISBN 0-06-020269-6 — ISBN 0-06-020270-X (lib. bdg.)
    ISBN 0-06-447095-4 (pbk.)
    [1. Rock music—Fiction. 2. Bands (Music)—Fiction.] I. Title.
PZ7.B61945Ch   1992   91-30706
[Fic]—dc20   CIP
                                                             AC

First Harper Trophy edition, 1993

Contents

Wind Song

The black Snake Wind came to me;
　The Black Snake Wind came to me,
Came and wrapped itself about,
　Came here running with its songs.

Pima Indian

Dear Everybody,

We miss you. Witch Baby is burying herself in mud again. But don't worry. Coyote is taking care of us the way you said he would. He is going to help me make Witch Baby some wings. Coyote is teaching me all about Indians. I am a deer, Witch Baby is a raven and Raphael is a dreaming obsidian elk. I hope the film is going well. We love you.

Cherokee Thunderbat

Wings

Cherokee Bat loved the canyons. Beach-
wood Canyon, lined with palm trees, hibiscus, bougainvillea and a row of candles
lit for the two old ladies who had been
killed by a hit-and-run, led to the Hollywood
sign or to the lake that changed colors under
a bridge of stone bears. Topanga Canyon

wound like a river to the sea past flower children, paintings of Indian goddesses and a restaurant where the tablecloths glowed purple-twilight and coyotes watched from among the leaves. Laurel Canyon had the ruins of Houdini's magic mansion, the country store where rock stars like Jim Morrison probably used to buy their beer, stained-glass Marilyn Monroes shining in the trees, leopard-spotted cars, gardens full of pink poison oleander and the Mediterranean villa on the hill where Joni Mitchell once lived, dreaming about clouds and carousels and guarded by stone lions. It also had the house built of cherry wood and antique windows where Cherokee lived with her family.

Cherokee always felt closer to animals in the canyons. Not just the stone lions and bears but the real animals—silver squirrels at the lake, deer, a flock of parrots that must have escaped their cages to find each other, peacocks screaming in gardens and the horses at Sunset Stables. Cherokee dreamed she was a horse with a mane the color of a smog-sunset, and she dreamed she was a bird with feathers like rainbows in oil puddles.

She would wake up and go to the mirror. She wanted to be faster, quieter, darker, shimmering. So she ran around the lake, up the trails, along winding canyon roads, trying not to make noise, barefoot so her feet would get tougher or in beaded moccasins when they hurt too much. Then she went back to the mirror. She was too naked. She wanted hooves, haunches, a beak, claws, wings.

There was a collage of dead butterflies on the wall of the canyon house where Cherokee lived with her almost-sister Witch Baby and the rest of their family. At night Cherokee dreamed the butterflies came to life, broke the glass and flew out at her in a storm, covering her with silky pollen. When she woke up she painted her dream. She searched for feathers everywhere—collected them in canyons and on beaches, comparing the shapes and colors, sketching them, trying to understand how they worked. Then she studied pictures of birds and pasted the feathers down in wing patterns. But it wasn't until Witch Baby began to bury herself that Cherokee decided to make the wings.

Witch Baby was Cherokee's almost-sister but they were very different. Cherokee's white-blonde hair was as easy to comb as water and she kept it in many long braids; Witch Baby's dark hair was a seaweed clump of tangles. It formed little angry balls that Witch Baby tugged at with her fingers until they pulled right out. Cherokee, who ran and danced, had perfect posture. Witch Baby's shoulders hunched up to her ears from years of creeping around taking candid photographs and from playing her drums. Cherokee wore white suede moccasins and turquoise and silver beads; Witch Baby's toes curled like snails inside her cowboy-boot roller-skates and she wore an assortment of whatever she could find until she decided she would rather wear mud.

One day, Witch Baby went into the backyard, took off all her clothes and began to roll around in the wet earth. She smeared mud everywhere, clumped handfuls into her hair, stuffed it in her ears, up her nostrils and even ate some. She slid around on her belly through the mud. Then she slid into the garden shed and lay there in the dark without moving.

Cherokee and Witch Baby's family, Weetzie Bat and My Secret Agent Lover Man, Brandy-

Lynn Bat and Dirk and Duck, were away in South America shooting a movie about magic. They had left Cherokee and Witch Baby under the care of their friend Coyote, but Cherokee hated to bother him. He lived on top of a hill and was always very busy with his chants and dances and meditative rituals. So Cherokee decided to try to take care of Witch Baby by herself. She went into the shed and said, "Witch Baby, come out. We'll go to Farmer's Market and get date shakes and look at the puppies in the pet store there and figure out a way to rescue them." But Witch Baby buried herself deeper in the mud.

"Witch Baby, come out and play drums for me," Cherokee said. "You are the most slinkster-jamming drummer girl and I want to dance." But Witch Baby shut her eyes and swallowed a handful of gritty dirt.

Cherokee heard Witch Baby's thoughts in her own head.

I am a seed in the slippery, silent, blind, breathless dark. I have no nose or mouth, ears or eyes to see. Just a skin of satin black and a secret green dream deep inside.

For hours, Cherokee begged Witch Baby to

come out. Finally she went into the house and called the boy who had been her best friend for as long as she could remember—Raphael Chong Jah-Love.

Raphael was practicing his guitar at the house down the street where he lived with his parents, Valentine and Ping Chong Jah-Love. Valentine and Ping were away in South America with Cherokee and Witch Baby's family working on the movie.

"Witch Baby is buried in mud!" Cherokee told Raphael when he answered the phone. "She won't come out of the shed. Could you ask her to play drums with us?"

"Witch Baby is the best drummer I know, Kee," Raphael said. "But she'll never play drums with us."

Raphael and Cherokee wanted to start a band but they needed a bass player and a drummer. Witch Baby had always refused to help them.

"Just ask her to play for you then, just once," Cherokee begged. "I am really worried about her."

So Raphael tossed his dreadlocks, put on his John Lennon sunglasses and rode his bicycle through sunlight and wind chimes and bird shadows to Cherokee's house.

He found Cherokee in the backyard among the fruit trees and roses knocking at the door of the shed. Witch Baby had locked herself in.

"Come out, Witch Baby," said Raphael. "I need to hear your drumming for inspiration. Even if you won't be in our band."

Cherokee kissed his powdered-chocolate-colored cheek. There was still no sound from inside the shed.

Cherokee and Raphael stood outside the shed for a long time. It got dark and stars came out, shining on the damp lawn.

"Let's go eat something," Raphael said. "Witch Baby will smell the food and come out."

They went inside and Cherokee took one of the frozen homemade pizzas that Weetzie had left them when the family went away, and put it in the oven. Raphael played an Elvis Presley record, lit some candles and made a salad. Cherokee opened all the windows—the stained-glass roses, the leaded-glass arches, the one that looked like rain—so Witch Baby would smell the melting cheese, hear it sizzle along with "Hound Dog" and come out of the mud shed. But when they had finished their pizza, there was still no sign of Witch Baby. They left two big slices of pizza in front of the shed. Then they set up Cherokee's tepee on the lawn, curled into their sleeping bags and told ghost stories until they fell asleep.

In the morning, the pizza looked as if it had been nibbled on by a mouse. Cherokee hoped the mouse had tangled hair, purple tilty eyes and curly toes, but the door of the shed was still locked.

Witch Baby would not come out of the mud shed. Cherokee finally decided she would have to ask Coyote what to do. With his wisdom and grace, he was the only one who would know how to bring Witch Baby out of the mud.

Early that morning, Cherokee took a bus into the hills where Coyote lived. She got off the bus and walked up the steep, winding streets to his shack. He was among the cactus plants doing his daily stretching, breathing and strengthening exercises when she found him. Below him the city was waking up under a layer of smog. Coyote turned his head slowly toward Cherokee and opened his eyes. Cherokee held her breath.

"Cherokee Bat," said Coyote in a voice that reminded her of sun-baked red rock, "are you all right? Why have you come?"

"Witch Baby is burying herself in mud," Cherokee told him. "She won't come out of the shed. We keep trying to help her but nothing works. I didn't know what else to do."

Coyote walked to the edge of the cactus garden and looked down at the layer of smog hovering over the city. He sighed and raised his deeply lined palms to the sky.

"No wonder Witch Baby is burying herself in mud," he said, looking out at the city drowning in smog. "There is dirt everywhere, real filth. We should not be able to see air. Air should be like the lenses of our eyes. And the sea . . . we should be able to swim in the sea; the sea should be like our tears and our sweat—clear and natural for us. There should be animals all around us—not hiding in the poison darkness, watching with their yellow eyes. Look at this city. Look what we have done."

Cherokee looked at the city and then she looked down at her hands. She felt small and pale and naked.

Coyote turned to Cherokee and put his hand on her shoulder. The early sun had filled the lines of his palm and now Cherokee felt it burning into her shoulder blade.

"The earth Witch Baby is burying herself in is purer than what surrounds us," Coyote said. "Maybe she feels it will protect her. Maybe she is growing up in it like a plant."

"But Coyote," Cherokee said. "She can't stay there forever in the mud shed. She hardly moves or eats anything."

Coyote looked back out at the city. Then he turned to Cherokee again and said softly, "I will help you to help Witch Baby. You must make her some wings."

A strong wind came. It dried the leaves to paper and the paper to flames like paint. Then it sent the flames through the papery hills and canyons, painting them red. It knocked over telephone poles and young trees and sent trash cans crashing in the streets. The wind made Cherokee's hair crackle with blue electric sparks. It made a kind of lemonade—cracking

· 14 ·

the glass chimes that hung in the lemon tree outside Cherokee's window into ice and tossing the lemons to the ground so they split open. It brought Cherokee the sea and the burning hills and faraway gardens. It brought her the days and nights early; she smelled the smoky dawn in the darkness, the damp dark while it was still light. And, finally, the wind brought her feathers.

She was standing with Coyote among the cactus and they were chanting to the animals hidden in the world below them, "You are all my relations." It was dawn and the wind was wild. Cherokee tried to understand what it was saying. There was a halo of blue sparks around her head.

"Wind, bring us the feathers that birds no longer need," Coyote chanted. "Hawk and dove. Tarred feathers of the gull. Shimmer peacock plumes. Jewel green of parrots and other kept birds. Witch Baby needs help leaving the mud."

The wind sounded wilder. Cherokee looked out at the horizon. As the sun rose, the sky filled with feathery pink clouds. Then it seemed as if the clouds were flying toward

Cherokee and Coyote. The rising sun flashed in their eyes for a moment, and as Cherokee stood, blind on the hilltop, she felt softness on her skin. The wind was full of feathers.

Small, bright feathers like petals, plain gray ones, feathers flecked with gleaming iridescent lights like tiny tropical waves. They swirled around Cherokee and Coyote, tickling their faces. Cherokee felt as if she could lift her arms and be carried away on wings of feathers and wind. She imagined flying over the city looking down at the tiny cars, palm trees, pools and lawns—all of it so ordered and calm—and not having to worry about anything. She imagined what her house would look like from above with its stained-glass skylights and rooftop deck, the garden with its fruit trees, roses, hot tub and wooden shed. And then she remembered Witch Baby slithering around in the mud. That was what this was all about—wings for Witch Baby.

The wind died down and the feathers settled around Cherokee and Coyote. They gathered the feathers, filling a big basket Coyote had brought from his shack.

"Now you can make the wings," Coyote said.

Cherokee looked at her hands.

Cherokee took wires and bent them into wing-shaped frames. Then she covered the frames with thin, stiff gauze, and over that she pasted the feathers the wind had brought. It took her a long time. She worked every day after school until late into the night. She hardly ate, did her homework or slept. At school she finally fell asleep on her desk and dreamed of falling into a feather bed. The dream-bed tore and feathers got into her nostrils and throat. She woke up coughing and the teacher sent her out of the room.

"What is wrong, Cherokee?" Raphael asked her on the phone when she wouldn't come over to play music with him. "You are acting as crazy as your sister."

But she only sighed and pasted down another feather in its place. "I can't tell you yet. Don't worry. You'll find out on Witch Baby's birthday."

The rain was like a green forest descending

over the city. Cherokee danced in puddles and caught raindrops off flower petals with her tongue. Her lungs didn't fill with smog when she ran. She loved the rain but she was worried, too. She was worried about Witch Baby getting sick out in the shed.

Cherokee brought blankets and a thermos of hot soup and put them outside the door. Witch Baby took the blankets and soup when no one was looking, but she didn't let Cherokee inside the shed.

When Witch Baby's birthday came, Cherokee and Raphael planned a big party for her. They made three kinds of salsa and a special dish of crumbled corn bread, green chiles, artichoke hearts, cheese and red peppers. They bought chips and soda and an ice-cream cake and decorated the house with tiny blinking colored lights, piñatas, big red balloons and black rubber bats. All their friends came, bringing incense, musical instruments, candles and flowers. Everyone ate, drank and danced to a tape Raphael had made of African music, salsa, zydeco, blues and soul. It was a perfect party except for one thing. Witch Baby wasn't there. She was still hiding in the shed.

Finally, Raphael got his guitar and began to play and sing some of Witch Baby's favorite songs—"Black Magic Woman," "Lust for Life," "Leader of the Pack" and "Wild Thing." Cherokee sang, too, and played her tambourine. Suddenly, the door opened and a boy came in. He was carrying a bass guitar and was dressed in baggy black pants, a white shirt buttoned to the collar and thick black shoes. A bandana was tied over his black hair. Everyone stopped and stared at him. Cherokee rubbed her eyes. It was Angel Juan Perez.

When Witch Baby was very little, she had fallen in love with Angel Juan, but he had had to go back to Mexico with his family. He still wrote to Witch Baby on her birthday and holidays and she said she dreamed about him all the time.

"Angel Juan!" Cherokee cried. She and Raphael ran to him and they all embraced.

"Where've you been?" Raphael asked.

"Mexico," said Angel Juan. "I've been playing music there since my family and I were sent back. I knew someday I'd get to see you guys again. And how is . . . ?"

"Witch Baby isn't so great," said Cherokee.

"She won't come out of the shed in back."

"What?" said Angel Juan. "Niña Bruja! My sweet, wild, purple-eyes!"

"Come and play some music for her," said Raphael. "Maybe she'll hear you and come out."

Witch Baby, huddling in the mud shed, smelled the food and saw colored lights blinking through the window. She even imagined the ice-cream cake glistening in the freezer. But nothing was enough to make her leave the shed until she heard a boy's voice singing a song.

"Niña Bruja," sang the voice.

Witch Baby stood up in the dark shed, shivering. Mud was caked all over her body, making her look like a strange animal with glowing purple eyes. It was raining when she stepped outside, and the water rinsed off the mud, leaving her naked and even colder. The voice drew her to the window of the house and she stared in.

Cherokee was the only one who noticed Witch Baby clinging to the windowsill and watching Angel Juan through the rain-streaked stained-glass irises. Cherokee ran and got a purple silk kimono robe embroidered with dragons, went out into the rain, slipped the robe on Witch Baby's hungry body, pried her fingers from the windowsill and took her hand. Hiding behind her tangled hair, Witch Baby followed Cherokee into the house as if she were in a trance.

Cherokee handed Witch Baby a pair of drumsticks and helped her tiptoe past everyone to the drums they had set up for her behind Raphael and Angel Juan. Witch Baby sat at her drums for a moment, biting her lip and staring at the back of Angel Juan's head. Then she lunged forward with her body and began to play.

Everyone turned to see what was happening. The drumming was powerful. It was almost impossible to believe it was coming through the body of a half-starved young girl who had been hiding in the mud for weeks. As Witch Baby played, a pair of multicolored wings descended from the ceiling. They shimmered in the lights as if they were in flight, reflecting the dawns and cities and sunsets they passed, then rested gently near Witch Baby's shoulders. Cherokee attached them there. The wings looked as if they had always been a part of Witch Baby's body, and the music she played made them tremble. Angel Juan turned to stare. Once everyone had caught their breath, they tossed their heads, stamped their feet, shook their hips and began to dance. Cherokee got her tambourine and joined the band.

When the song was over, Cherokee brought out the ice-cream cake burning with candles and everyone sang "Happy Birthday, dear Witch Baby." It was hard for Cherokee to recognize her almost-sister. Glowing from music, and magical in the Cherokee wind-wings, Witch Baby was beautiful. Angel Juan could not take his eyes off her.

After she had blown out all the candles, he came up and took her hand. "Niña Bruja," he said, "I've missed you so much."

Witch Baby looked up at Angel Juan's smooth, brown face with the high cheekbones, the black-spark eyes. The last time she had seen him, he was a tiny blur of a boy.

"Dance with me," he said.

Witch Baby looked down at her bare, curly toes. There was still mud under her toenails, but the wings made her feel safe.

"Dance with me, Niña Bruja," Angel Juan said again. He put his hands on Witch Baby's shoulders, hunched tightly beneath the wings, and she relaxed. Then he took one of her hands, uncurling the fingers, and began to dance with her in the protective shade of many feathers. Witch Baby pressed her head of wild hair against Angel Juan's clean, white shirt.

Everyone clapped for them, then found partners and joined in. Cherokee stood watching. She remembered how Witch Baby and Angel Juan had played together when they were very young, how Witch Baby had covered her walls with pictures she had taken of him, how she never bit her nails or pulled at her snarlballs or hissed or spit when he was around. Then he had had to leave so suddenly when his family was sent back to Mexico.

Now, seeing them dancing together, the nape of Angel Juan's neck exposed as he bent to hold Witch Baby, the black flames of her hair pressed against his chest, Cherokee felt like crying.

Raphael came up to Cherokee and took her hands. For almost their whole lives, Cherokee and Raphael had been inseparable, but tonight Cherokee felt something new. It was something tight and slidey in her stomach, something burning and shivery in her spine; it was like having hearts beating in her throat and knees. Raphael had never looked so much like a lion with his black eyes and mane of dreadlocks.

"The wings are beautiful, Kee," Raphael said. "They are the best gift anyone could give to Witch Baby." He lifted Cherokee's hands into the light and examined them. "How did you do it?" he asked.

"Love."

"You are magic," Raphael said. "I've known that since we were babies, but now your magic is very strong. I think you are going to have to be careful."

"Careful?" said Cherokee. "What do you mean?"

"Never mind," said Raphael. "I just got a funny feeling. I just want things to stay like this forever." And he stroked Cherokee's long, yellow braids, but he didn't put his arms around her the way he had always done before.

Song of Encouragement

Within my bowl there lies
Shining dizziness,
Bubbling drunkenness.

There are great whirlwinds
Standing upside down above us.
They lie within my bowl.

A great bear heart,
A great eagle heart,
A great hawk heart,
A great twisting wind—
All these have gathered here
And lie within my bowl.

Now you will drink it.

Papago Indian

Dear Everybody,

Witch Baby is fine! Angel Juan came back.
He got here on Witch Baby's birthday! That
was her best present but I also gave her some
wings Coyote helped me make. She looks like
she will fly away. Angel Juan moved in with
Raphael and Witch Baby is still sleeping in
the garden shed but she isn't doing the mud
thing anymore. We started a band called The
Goat Guys. We are going to play out soon, I
think. Raphael is the most slinkster-cool
singer and guitar player. We all send our
love.

Cherokee

Haunches

After Witch Baby's birthday, Cherokee, Raphael, Witch Baby and Angel Juan decided to form a band called The Goat Guys. Every day, when Angel Juan got home from the restaurant where he worked and the others from school, they practiced in Raphael's garage with posters of Bob Marley,

The Beatles, The Doors and John Lennon and a painted velvet tapestry of Elvis on the walls around them. Witch Baby sat at her drums, her purple eyes fierce, her skinny arms pounding out the beat; Angel Juan pouted and swayed as he played his bass, and Raphael sang in a voice like Kahlúa and milk, swinging his dreadlocks to the sound of his guitar. Cherokee, whirling with her tambourine, imagined she could see their music like fireworks—flashing flowers and fountains of light exploding in the air around them.

One night, Cherokee and Raphael were walking through the streets of Hollywood. Because it had just rained and was almost Christmas, a twinkling haze covered the whole city.

They passed stucco bungalows with Christmas trees shining in the windows and roses in the courtyard gardens. They stopped to catch raindrops off the rose petals with their tongues.

"What does this smell like?" Cherokee asked, sniffing a yellow rose.

"Lemonade."

"And the orange ones smell like peaches."

Raphael put his face inside a white rose. "Rain," he said.

They walked on Melrose with its neon, lovers, frozen yogurt and Italian restaurants, Santa Monica with its thin boys on bus-stop benches, lonely hot dog stands, auto repair shops where the cars glowed with fluorescent raindrops, Sunset with its billboard mouths calling you toward the sea, and Hollywood where golden lights arched from movie palace to movie palace over fake snow, pavement stars, ghetto blasters, drug dealers, pinball players and women in high-heeled pumps walking in Marilyn's footprints in front of the Chinese Theater.

Cherokee and Raphael made shadow animals with their hands when they came to bare walls. They stopped for ice-cream cones. Cherokee heard Raphael's voice singing in her head as she sucked a marshmallow out of her scoop of rocky road.

"We are ready to play out," she told him. They were hopping from star to star on Hollywood Boulevard.

"I don't know. I'm not sure I want to deal

with the whole nightclub scene," he said.

"But it would be good for people to hear you." She looked at him. Raindrops had fallen off some of the roses they had been smelling and sparkled in his dreadlocks. He was wearing a denim jacket and jeans and he stepped lightly on his toes as if he weren't quite touching the ground.

He shrugged. "I don't think it's so important. I like to just play for our friends."

"But other people need our music, too. Let's just send the tape around," Cherokee said. She looked up and pointed to the spotlights fanning across the cloudy sky. "I think you are a star, Raphael. You're my star. I'll send the tapes for us."

He shook his head so his hair flew out, scattering the drops of rain. "Okay, okay. You can if you really want to."

Let's not be afraid, Cherokee thought. Let's not be afraid of anything that can't really hurt us. She grabbed his wrist and they ran across the street as the red stoplight hand flashed.

———

Cherokee sent Goat Guy tapes to night-clubs around the city. She put a photograph that Witch Baby had taken of the band on the front of the cassette. Zombo of Zombo's Rockin' Coffin called her and said he could book a show just before Christmas.

When Cherokee told Raphael, he got very quiet. "I'm not sure we're ready," he said, but she kissed him and told him they were a rockin' slink-chunk, slam-dunk band and that it would be fine.

On the night of the first show, Raphael lit a cigarette.

"What are you doing?" Cherokee said, try-ing to grab it out of his hand. They were sit-ting backstage at the Coffin. Raphael coughed but then he took another hit.

"Leave me alone," he said. He got up and paced back and forth.

Angel Juan and Witch Baby came with Witch Baby's drums.

"What's wrong, man?" Angel Juan asked, but Raphael just took another puff of smoke.

Cherokee had never seen him look like this. There were dark circles under his eyes and his skin seemed faded. And he had never told her to leave him alone before.

Cherokee kissed Raphael's cheek and went to the front of the club. It was decorated with pieces of black fabric, sickly-looking Cupids, candles and fake, greenish lilies. The people seated at the tables had the same coloring as the flowers. They were slumped over their drinks waiting for the music to begin.

Cherokee turned to see a short, fat man in a tuxedo staring at her. His chubby fingers with their longish nails were wrapped around a tall glass of steaming blue liquid.

"Aren't you a little young to be in my club?"

"I'm in the band," Cherokee said.

"You sure don't look like a Goat Guy." He eyed her up and down and wiped his mouth with the back of his hand.

Cherokee glared at him.

"Sorry to stare. I always stare at how girls do their makeup. It's a business thing. I like that blue line around your eyes."

She started to edge away.

"I used to be an undertaker before I

opened this place. Still got family in the business. Maybe you could come with me sometime and make up a few faces. You did your eyes real nice."

Cherokee could smell Zombo's breath. Her stomach churned and tumbled. "I better go get ready," she said, feeling him watching as she walked backstage.

When the band came on, Cherokee saw Zombo leering up at her with his hands in his pants pockets. She saw the rest of the hollow-eyed audience lurched forward on their elbows and guzzling their drinks. Standing there in the spotlight, she felt an icy wave crash in her chest and she knew that she was not going to be able to play or sing or dance. She could tell that the rest of The Goat Guys were frozen too. Witch Baby lost a drumstick right away and started to jump up and down, gnashing her teeth. When Angel Juan played the wrong chords, he frowned and rolled his eyes. But it was Raphael who suffered more than anyone that night. He stood trembling on the stage with his dreadlocks hanging in his face. His voice strained from his throat so that Cherokee could hardly recognize it.

The Coffin crowd began to hiss and spit. Some threw cigarette butts and maraschino cherries at the stage. When a cherry hit Raphael in the temple, he looked helplessly around him, then turned and disappeared behind the black curtain. Witch Baby thrust her middle finger into the air and waved it around.

"Clutch pigs!" she shouted.

Then, she, Cherokee and Angel Juan followed Raphael backstage, ducking to miss the objects flying through the air at them.

Raphael hardly spoke to anyone after Zombo's Coffin. He didn't want to rehearse or play basketball, surf or talk or eat. He lay in his room under the hieroglyphics he and Cherokee had once painted on his wall, listened to Jimi Hendrix, Led Zeppelin and The Doors and smoked more and more cigarettes. Cherokee came over with chocolates and oranges and strands of beads she had strung, but he only glared at her and turned up the volume on his stereo. She didn't know what to say.

When Christmas came, Cherokee, Witch Baby and Angel Juan planned a party to cheer Raphael up and keep them all from missing their families. Angel Juan drove his red pickup truck downtown at dawn to a place by the railroad tracks and came back with a pink snow-sugared tree that Witch Baby and Cherokee decorated with feathers, beads and miniature globes; Kachina, Barbie and Japanese baby dolls; and Mexican skeletons. They filled the rooms with pine branches, red berries, pink poinsettias, tiny white lights, strands of colored stars and salsa and gospel music. They baked cookies in the shapes of hieroglyphics and Indian symbols and breads in the shapes of angels and mermaids.

On Christmas Eve they made hot cinnamon cider, corn bread, yams, salad and cranberry salmon and invited Raphael over. The table was an island of candles and flowers and cascading mountains of food floating in the dark sea of the room.

And we are the stars in the sky, Cherokee thought, seeing all their faces circling the table.

Raphael was hunched in his chair playing with his food. She had never seen him look so far away from her.

After dinner they opened presents in front of the fire. Big packages had arrived from their families—leather backpacks, woven blankets, painted saints and angels, mysterious stones, beaded scarves and candelabra in the shapes of pink mermaids and blue doves. Coyote, who had been invited but did not want to leave his hilltop, had painted Indian birth charts for everyone—Cherokee the deer, Witch Baby the raven, Raphael and Angel Juan the elks. Everyone loved their presents except for Raphael. He didn't seem to care about anything.

"Raphael," Cherokee whispered, "what do you want me to give you for Christmas?"

The fire crackled and embers showered down. The air smelled of pine and cinnamon.

Raphael just stared at her body without saying anything, his eyes reflecting the flames, and Cherokee was glad she was wrapped in one of the woven blankets her family had sent.

The next day Cherokee went to see Coyote. He was watering the vegetables he grew among his cactus plants.

"Our first show was terrible," she told him.

"Yes?"

"Raphael is very upset. I don't know what to do."

"You must practice."

"He won't even pick up his guitar."

"What did you come to me for, Cherokee?"

"I was wondering," she said, "if maybe you would help me make something for Raphael. The wings helped Witch Baby so much."

Coyote squinted at the sun. "And what do you think would help Raphael?"

"Not wings. Maybe some goat pants would help. Then he'd feel like a Goat Guy and not be so scared on stage. He's really good, Coyote. He just gets stage fright."

Coyote sighed and shook his head.

"Please, Coyote. Just one more gift. I am really worried that Raphael will hurt himself. It's kind of hard for him with his parents away and everything."

Coyote sighed again. "I did promise all your parents I would help you," he said. "But I must think about this. Go now. I must think alone."

So Cherokee went to Raphael's house, where she found him lying on his bed in the dark listening to Jimi Hendrix and smoking a cigarette. She sat cross-legged beside him. The moonlight fell across the blankets in tiger stripes.

"What?" he growled.

"Nothing. I just came to be with you."

Raphael turned his back, and when she tried to stroke his shoulder through the thin T-shirt, he jerked away.

"Come on, Raphael, let's play some music."

"I am playing music," he said, turning up the volume on the stereo.

"We can't just give up."

"I can."

Cherokee wanted to touch him. She felt the tingling sliding from her scalp down her spine and back again. "We need practice, that's all. We're just not used to playing live, and that club wasn't the right place anyway." As she spoke, she loosened her braids, tossing her gold hair near his face like a cloud of flowers.

He stirred a little, awakened by her, then smashed his cigarette into an Elvis ashtray. She noticed how thick the veins were in his arms, the strain in his throat, the width of his knees in his jeans. He seemed older, suddenly. The small brown body she had grown up with, sprawled beside on warm rocks, painted pictures on, slept beside in her tepee, was no longer so familiar. He reached out and barely stroked the blonde bouquet of her hair with the back of his hand. Then, suddenly, he grabbed her wrists and pulled her toward him. Cherokee didn't recognize the flat, dark look in Raphael's eyes. She pulled away, twisting her wrists so they slipped from his hands.

"I have to go," she said.

"Cherokee!" His voice sounded hoarse.

"I'll talk to you tomorrow." Cherokee backed out of the room. When she got outside she heard howling and the trees looked like shadow cats ready to spring. She thought there were men hiding in the dark, watching her run down the street in her thin, white moccasins.

The next day, after school, Cherokee went to see Coyote again. He was standing in his cactus garden as if waiting for her, but when she went to greet him he didn't say anything. He turned away, shut his eyes and began to hum and chant. The sounds hissed like fire, became deep water, then blended together, as hushed as smoke. Cherokee felt the sounds in her own chest—imagined flames and rivers and clouds filling her so that she wanted to dance them. But she stayed very still and listened.

Cherokee and Coyote stood on the hillside for a long time. Cherokee tried not to be impatient, but an hour passed, then another, and even Coyote's chants were not mesmerizing enough to make her forget that she had to find a way to make goat pants or something for Raphael. It was getting dark.

Coyote turned his broad face up to the sky and kept chanting. It seemed as if the darkening sky were touching him, Cherokee thought, pressing lightly against his eyelids and palms, as if the leaves in the trees were shivering to be near him, even the pebbles on the hillside shifting, and then she saw that pebbles were moving, sliding down, the leaves were shaking and singing in harsh, throaty voices. Or something was singing. Something was coming.

The goats clambered down sideways toward Cherokee and Coyote. A whirlwind of dust and fur. Their jaws and beards swung from side to side; their eyes blinked.

"I guess these are the real goat guys," Cherokee said.

Coyote opened his eyes and the goats gathered around his legs. He laid his palms on each of their skulls, one at a time, in the bony hollow between the horns. They were all suddenly very quiet.

Coyote turned and the goats followed him into his shack, butting each other as they went. Cherokee stood in the doorway and watched as Coyote lit candles and sheared the thick, shaggy fur off the goat haunches. They did not complain. When he was done with one, the next would come, not even flinching at the buzz of the electric shears. The dusty fur piled up on the floor of the shack, and when the last and smallest goat had been shorn, they all scrambled away out the door, up the hillside and into the night.

Cherokee watched their naked backsides disappearing into the brush. She wanted to thank them but she didn't know what to say. How do you thank a bare-bottomed goat who is rushing up a mountain after he has just given you his fur? she wondered.

Coyote stood in the dim shack. Cherokee noticed that his hair was even shinier with perspiration. She had never seen him sweat before. He frowned at the pile of fur.

"Well, Cherokee Bat," Coyote said, "here is your fur. Use it well. The fur and the feathers were gifts that the animals gave you without death, untainted. But think of the animals that have died for their hides, and for their beauty and power. Think of them, too, when you sew for your friends."

Cherokee gathered the fur in bags and thanked Coyote. She wanted to leave right away without even asking him how to go about making the haunches. There was a mute, remote look on his face as if he were trying to remember something.

When Cherokee got home, she thought of Coyote's expression and blinked to send the image away. It frightened her. She washed the fur, pulling out nettles and leaves, watching the dark water swirl down the drain. The next day she dried the fur in the sun. But she did not know what to do next.

For nights she lay awake, trying to decide how to make haunches. She dreamed of goats dancing in misty forest glades, rising on their hind legs as they danced, wreathed with flowers, baring their teeth, drunk on flower pollen, staggering, leaping. She dreamed of girls too—pale and naked, being chased by the goats. The girls tried to cover their nakedness but the heavy, hairy goat heads swung toward them, teeth chewing flowers, eyes menacing, the forest closing in around, leaves chiming like bells.

Cherokee woke up clutching the sheets around her body. The room smelled of goat, and she got up to open the windows. As she leaned out into the night, filling herself with the fragrance of the canyon, she thought of Raphael's heavy dreadlocks, the cords of hair like fur. She had spent hours winding beads and feathers into his hair and her own. Now she loosened her braids.

She knew, suddenly, how she would make the pants.

Cherokee braided and braided strands of fur together. Then she attached the braids to a pair of Raphael's old jeans. She put extra fur along the hips so the pants really looked like shaggy goat legs. She made a tail with the rest of the fur. When she was finished, Cherokee brought the haunches to Raphael's house and left them at the door in a box covered with leaves and flowers.

That night he called her: "I'm coming over," and hung up.

She went to the mirror, took off her T-shirt and looked at her naked body. Too thin, she thought, too pale. She wished she were dark like the skins of certain cherries and had bigger breasts. Quickly she dressed again, brushed her hair and touched some of Weetzie's gardenia perfume to the place at her throat where she could feel her heart.

When Raphael came to the door, Cherokee saw him through the peephole at first—silhouetted against the night with his long, ropy hair, his chest bare under his denim jacket, his fur legs.

Cherokee opened the door and he walked in heavily, strutting, not floating. The tail swung behind him as he went straight to Cherokee's room and turned off the light. She hesitated at the door.

"They look good," she said.

Raphael stared at her. "Things are different now." His voice was hoarse. "Come here."

His teeth and eyes flashed, reflecting the light from the hallway. He was like a forest creature who didn't belong inside.

Cherokee tried to breathe. She wanted to go to him and stroke his head. She wanted to paint red and silver flowers on his chest and then curl up beside him in her tepee the way she used to do. But he was right. Things were different now.

Then, without even realizing it, she was

standing next to him. They were still almost the same height. She could smell him—cocoa, a light basketball sweat. She could see his lips.

All their lives, Cherokee and Raphael had given each other little kisses, but this kiss was like a wind from the desert, a wind that knocks over candles so that flowers catch fire, a wind, or like a sunset in the desert casting sphinx shadows on the sand, a sunset, or like a shivering in the spine of the earth. They collapsed, their hands sliding down each other's arms. Then they were reeling over and over among the feathers and dried flowers that covered Cherokee's floor. She remembered how they had rolled down hills together, tangling and untangling, the smell of crushed grass and coconut sun lotion and barbecue smoke all mixed up in their heads. Then, when she had rolled against him, she hardly felt it—they were like one body. Now each touch stung and sparkled. He grasped her hair in his hand and kissed her neck, then pressed his face between her breasts as if he were trying to get inside to her heart.

"White Dawn," he whispered. "Cherokee White Dawn."

Suddenly she couldn't swallow—the air thick around her like waves of dark dreadlocks—and she pushed him away.

Raphael put his hands on his stomach. He glared at her. "What are you doing?"

Cherokee ran out of the room, out of the house, to the garden shed where Witch Baby was practicing her drums. Cherokee leaned her head against the wall, feeling the pounding go through her body.

"What's wrong with you?" Witch Baby asked when she had finished playing.

"Can I stay here tonight?"

"Why? Is Raphael being a wild thing?"

"I just don't feel like being in the house," Cherokee said.

"*Sure!*" said Witch Baby. "I bet it's because of Raphael. I just hope you use birth control like Weetzie told us."

Cherokee frowned and started to turn away.

"I guess you can stay if you want," Witch Baby said.

Cherokee curled up next to Witch Baby but she didn't sleep all night. She lay awake with the moon pouring over her through the shed window, bleaching her skin even whiter. Sometimes she thought she heard Witch Baby's hoarse voice singing her a mysterious lullaby, but she wasn't sure.

After that, Cherokee was afraid to see Raphael, but he called her a few days later and said there would be a rehearsal at his house the next day. It was the first time he had suggested that they play music since Zombo's Coffin.

Raphael wore the fur pants. He didn't say much to Cherokee but he sang and played better than ever. When they were done, he said, "I booked a gig for us."

"Where at?" Angel Juan asked, peering over the top of his sunglasses.

"I thought you didn't want to play," Witch Baby said.

"It's at The Vamp. We'd be opening for The Devil Dogs."

"Sounds kind of creepy!" Cherokee said, but she was glad that Raphael wanted to play again.

"The owner, Lulu, heard our tape. She is really into us." Raphael stomped over to the mirror, puffed out his chest and modeled the fur pants. "The Goat Guys are ready for anything now."

Lulu was tall and black-cherry skinned with waves of dark hair and large breasts. She moved gracefully in her short red dress.

"How do you like the club?" Lulu asked Raphael, brushing his arm with her fingertips.

The Vamp was dark with black skull candles burning and stuffed animal heads on the walls. Cherokee shivered.

"It's a great setup. Thanks, a lot," he said, looking at Lulu's lips as if he were in a trance.

Lulu smiled. "I think you'll be just great here, honey," she said. "Let me know if you need anything."

She walked away, shifting her hips precisely from side to side. Raphael watched her go.

"Raphael!" Cherokee said. A stuffed deer head had its glass eyes fixed on her.

"Let's do a sound check," Raphael said to his cigarette.

Maybe it was the fact that they had been rehearsing or that after the first show it just got easier, or maybe it was the goat pants. Or maybe, Cherokee thought, it was the anger Raphael felt toward her after the night in her bedroom—the power of that. Whatever the reason, Raphael was not the frightened boy who had left the Rockin' Coffin stage before the first song was over.

He strutted, he staggered, he jerked, he swirled his dreadlocks and his tail. He bared his teeth. He touched his bare chest. His sweat flew into the audience.

The audience howled, panted and crowded nearer to the stage, their faces bony as the wax skull candles they held above their heads. The flame shadows danced across Raphael's face.

With the heat pressing toward them and Raphael's bittersweet voice and reeling body moving them, Angel Juan, Witch Baby and Cherokee began to play better than they had ever played before. Cherokee felt as if the band were becoming one lashing, shimmery creature that the room full of people in leather wanted to devour. Someone reached up and pulled at her skirt, and she whirled away from the edge of the stage. The room was spinning but even as she felt hunted, trapped, about to be devoured by the crowd at the foot of the stage, she also felt free, flickering above them, able to hypnotize, powerful. The power of the trapped animal who is, for that moment, perfect, the hunter's only thought and desire.

When the set was over, the band slipped backstage away from the shrieks and the bones and the burning. Raphael turned to Cherokee, drenched and feverish. She was afraid he would turn away again but instead he took her face in his hands and kissed her cheeks.

"Thank you, Cherokee White Dawn," he murmured.

Then they were running, holding hands and running out of the club. They ran through the streets of Hollywood but Cherokee hardly noticed the fallen stars, the neon cocktail glasses. They could have been anywhere—a forest, a desert—running in the moon-shadow of the sphinx, a jungle where the night was green. They could have been goats, horses, wildcats. They could have been dreaming or running through someone else's dream.

They ran to Raphael's house. Cherokee felt a metallic pinch between her eyes, something hot and wet on her upper lip. She touched her nose and looked at her fingers. "I'm bleeding."

Raphael helped her lie down on his bed. He brought her a wet cloth and pressed it against her nose. "Keep your head back."

"I get too excited, I guess."

As he cradled her head in one hand, he began kissing her throat, the insides of her elbows and wrists for a long time. Then he kissed her forehead and temples. "Is it better?"

She moved the cloth away and sat up. It was dark in the room but the animals, pyramids, eyes and lotus flowers glimmered on the moonlit wall. Cherokee and Raphael were both sweaty and tangled. She could smell his chocolate, her vanilla-gardenia, and something else that was both mingling together.

"Coyote told me about Indian women who fell in love with men because of their flute playing and got nosebleeds when they heard the music because they were so excited," Cherokee said.

"Does it work with a guitar?"

"It works when I look at you."

He touched her face. "You're okay now, I think. . . . I miss you, Cherokee. I want to wake up with you in the morning the way we used to. But different. It's different now."

It was different. It was light-filled red waves breaking on a beach again and again—a salt-stung fullness. It was being the waves and riding the waves. The bed lifted, the house and the lawn and the roses and the street and the night, one ocean rocking them, tossing them, an ocean of liquid coral roses.

Afterward, Cherokee was washed ashore with her head on his chest. She could hear the echo of herself inside of him.

Song of the Fallen Deer

At the time of the White Dawn;
   At the time of the White Dawn,
I arose and went away.
   At Blue Nightfall I went away.

I ate the thornapple leaves
   And the leaves made me dizzy.
I drank the thornapple flowers
   And the drink made me stagger.

The hunter, Bow-Remaining,
   He overtook and killed me,
Cut and threw my horns away.
   The hunter, Reed-Remaining,
He overtook and killed me,
   Cut and threw my feet away.

Now the flies become crazy
   And they drop with flapping wings.
The drunken butterflies sit
   With opening and shutting wings.

Pima Indian

Dear Everybody,

The Goat Guys played at a club called The Vamp and we jammed. I wish you could have seen us. I made Raphael these cool fur pants so he really looks like a Goat Guy. It's getting warm and I'm having a little trouble concentrating on school. But don't worry. We're all doing our work and we only play in clubs on weekends mostly. Thanks for your letter.

Love,
Cherokee Goat-Bat

Horns

Cherokee noticed that the air was beginning to change, becoming powder-sugary with pollen as if invisible butterfly wings and flower petals were brushing against her skin. It was getting warmer. The light was different now—dappled greenish-gold and watery. After school, The Goat Guys would run,

bicycle and roller-skate home to play basketball or, when Angel Juan got back from the
restaurant wearing his white busboy shirt that
smelled of soup and bread and tobacco, they
would all ride to the beach in his red truck and
surf or play volleyball on the sand until sunset. At night they rehearsed. It was hard for
them to think about homework or studying
when they were getting so many calls to play in
clubs. Everyone wanted to see the wild goat
singer, the winged witch drummer, the dark,
graceful angel bass player and the spinning
blonde tambourine dancer.

After rehearsals, or on weekends after the
shows, Cherokee and Raphael stayed together in his bed or her tepee. She hardly
slept. There was a constant tossing and tangling of their bodies, a constant burning heat.
She remembered how she had slept before—a
caterpillar in a cocoon, muffled and peaceful.
Now she woke up fragile and shaky like some
new butterfly whose wings are still translu-
cent green, easy to tear and awaiting their
color. All day she smelled Raphael on her
skin. Her eyes were stinging and glazed and

her head felt heavy. A slow ache spread through her hips and thighs.

"Cherokee and Raphael are doing it!" Witch Baby sang.

Cherokee tried to ignore her.

"Aren't you? Aren't you doing it?"

"Shut up, Witch."

"You are! I hear you guys. And you look all tired all the time."

"Stop it, Witch. You shouldn't talk. Why would you want to move out into the shed? I bet I know what you and Angel Juan do out there."

Witch Baby was quiet. She gnawed her fingernails and pulled at a snarl-ball in her hair. Right away, Cherokee wished she hadn't said anything. She realized that Witch Baby wouldn't tease her if Witch and Angel Juan were doing the same thing.

Witch Baby bared her teeth at Cherokee. "I'm writing to Weetzie and telling!" she said as she roller-skated away.

Cherokee watched Angel Juan and Witch Baby more closely after that. She saw how Angel Juan tousled Witch Baby's hair and picked her up sometimes. But he did it like an older brother. When Witch Baby looked at Angel Juan, her tilty eyes turned the color of amethysts and got so big that her pointed face seemed smaller than ever.

One day, while The Goat Guys were rehearsing, Raphael went over and touched Cherokee's hair. It was only a light touch but it was so charged that tiny electric sparks seemed to flare up. Witch Baby stopped drumming. Angel Juan's eyes were hidden behind his sunglasses. Witch Baby looked at him. Then she got up and ran out of the room.

Cherokee followed her into the garden. "What is it, Witch?" she asked.

Witch Baby didn't answer.

"I see how he looks at you when you wear your wings and play drums for him. I think he's just afraid of his feelings."

Witch Baby shrugged and chewed her fingernails.

"Tell me about Angel Juan."

Witch Baby didn't say anything about Angel Juan out loud, but Cherokee could tell what she was thinking.

He is a dangerous flamenco shadow dancer and a tiny boy playing music in the gutter. His soul sounds like my drums and looks like doves. He is fireworks. He is the black-haired angel playing his bass on the top of the tree, on the top of the cake. I want him to see the flowers in my eyes and hear the songs in my hands.

After a show at The Vamp, some girls followed Raphael backstage. They wanted to stroke his fur pants, they told him, giggling. One kept flicking out her tongue like a snake. They wore black bras and black leather miniskirts.

Cherokee stood with her arms crossed on her chest, watching them. Then she noticed that Angel Juan was standing in the same position with a frown on his face that matched her own. He turned and stalked out of the club, and Witch Baby came and stood beside Cherokee.

"All the girls pay attention to Raphael but Angel Juan is a slinkster-cool bass player and beautiful, too," Cherokee said.

"Ever since you made Raphael those goat pants, he's been acting like the only person in the band," Witch Baby said. Then she added, "You never made anything for Angel Juan."

Cherokee wished the girls would leave Raphael alone, take their hands off his hips and their breasts away from his face. But she thought he was happier lately than he had ever been and he would hold her in the tepee that night and sing songs he had made up about her until the images of the girls drifted out of her head and she fell into a sleep of running animals and breaking lily-filled waves. But what about Witch Baby? She would be curled up in the shed under the bass drum, alone. She would dream of Angel Juan's obsidian hair and deer face, reach for him and find a hollow drum. What about Angel Juan? Cherokee thought. He would be waiting outside for them by his red truck with a frown on his face. He would drive home with swerves and startling stops. He would not look at any of them, especially Witch Baby. He was the only Goat Guy Cherokee had not made a present for.

What should I do for Angel Juan? Cherokee wondered. I will ask Coyote.

Cherokee, Witch Baby and Raphael went out to meet Angel Juan at his truck.

"We were hot tonight," said Raphael.

Angel Juan turned to him. "What makes you think you are such a star all of a sudden, man?"

"I said *we*. I can't help it if the girls like me," Raphael said, tossing his dreadlocks back over his bare shoulders.

"They might like me too if I shook my hips at them like some stripper chick."

"Maybe they would." Raphael grinned and swiveled his hips in the goat pants. "Why don't you, man? Too freaked out?"

That was when Angel Juan made a fist and hit Raphael in the stomach under his ribs. Raphael staggered backward, staring at Angel Juan as if he weren't quite sure what had just happened.

Cherokee put her arms around Raphael. I will have to go back to Coyote, she thought.

Cherokee asked Coyote if she could go running with him around the lake. It was a morning of green mist, and needles of sun were coming through the pines. Cherokee had to run at her very fastest pace to keep up with Coyote's long legs. She glanced over at his profile—the proud nose, the flat dreamy eyelids, the trail of blue-black hair.

"Coyote . . . " Cherokee panted.

"We are running, Cherokee Bat," Coyote said. "Keep running. Think of making your legs long. Think of deer and wind."

When they had circled the lake twice, Cherokee leaned against a tree to catch her breath. She felt as if Coyote had been testing her, forcing her forward.

"Coyote," she said. "I have to ask you something."

Coyote was tall. He never smiled. He had chosen to live alone, to work and mourn and see visions, in a nest above the smog. The animals came to him when he spoke their names. He was full of grace, wisdom and mystery. He had seen his people die, wasted on their lost lands. Cherokee had never seen his tears but she thought they were probably like drops of turquoise or liquid silver, like tiny moons and stars showering from his eyes. She knew that he had more important things to do than give her gifts. But still, she needed him. And she had gone this far.

"Coyote, Angel Juan is jealous of Raphael. He's shy around girls—even Witch Baby, and I know he loves her. Witch Baby is jealous of how Raphael is with me. She wants Angel Juan to treat her the same way. Angel Juan is the only one of The Goat Guys I haven't made anything for," Cherokee blurted out. Then she stopped. Coyote was eyeing her.

"Cherokee Bat," he said. "The birds have given you feathers for Witch Baby. The goats have given you fur for Raphael Chong Jah-Love. What do you want now?"

"I want the horns on your shelf for Angel Juan," Cherokee whispered.

She was braced against the tree, and she realized that she was waiting for something, for thunder to crack suddenly or for the ground to shake. But nothing happened. The morning was quiet—the early sun coaxing the fragrance from the pines and the earth. Coyote did not even blink. He was silent for a while. Then he spoke.

"My people are great runners, Cherokee. They go on ritual runs. Before these they abstain from eating fatty meat and from sexual relations. These things can drain us."

Cherokee looked down at the ground and shrugged. "What do you mean?"

"You know what I mean. You are very young still. So is Raphael. Angel Juan and Witch Baby are both very young. You must be careful. While your parents are away, I am responsible. Use your wisest judgment and protect yourself."

"We do. I do," Cherokee said. "Weetzie told me and Witch Baby all about that stuff. But this is about Angel Juan. We all have what we want, but it's been harder for him his whole life and now he's the only one without a present."

"There is power, great power," Coyote said. "You do not understand it yet."

"I am careful," Cherokee insisted. "Besides, if I haven't been responsible, it doesn't have to do with you or with the wings and haunches. I just want the horns for Angel Juan so he won't feel left out."

"I cannot do any more for you. You'll have to make something else for Angel Juan. I cannot give you the horns."

"Coyote . . . "

"I want you to try to get more sleep," Coyote said. "If you want to find the trail, if you want to find yourself, you must explore your dreams alone. You must grow at a slow pace in a dark cocoon of loneliness so you can fly like wind, like wings, when you awaken."

I'm awake now, Cherokee wanted to shout. I'm a woman already and you want to keep me a child. You want us all to be children.

But instead she turned, jumped on Raphael's red bicycle and rode down the hill, away from the lake, away from Coyote.

Cherokee could not stop thinking about the horns. Why was Coyote so afraid of giving them to her? She had always known inside that the wings and the haunches were not just feathers and fur. The horns must have even greater power.

Cherokee rode home and found Witch Baby practicing her drums in the shed.

"I tried to get a present for Angel Juan," Cherokee said. "But Coyote won't help me. I don't know what to do."

"What about those goat horns you were talking about?"

Cherokee played with one of her braids. "Coyote said the horns have a lot of power. He's afraid to give them to us."

Witch Baby crunched up her face. "It's not fair. Coyote helped you get presents for me and Raphael." She was quiet for a moment. "I wonder what's so special about the horns," she said. "I want to find out."

"Witch, don't do anything creepy," Cherokee said. "Coyote is like a dad to us and he is very powerful."

Witch Baby pulled a tangle-ball out of her hair, looked at it and growled. Watching her, Cherokee wished she hadn't said anything about the horns. Witch Baby might do something. But at the same time Cherokee was curious. What would happen to The Goat Guys if they had the magic horns?

I don't need to know, Cherokee told herself. I'll think of something else for Angel Juan. And Witch Baby is only a little girl. She won't be able to do anything Coyote doesn't want her to do.

Witch Baby was little. She was so small that she was able to slip in through the window of Coyote's shack one night. Witch Baby was very quiet when she wanted to be, and very fast—so quiet and fast that she was able to take the goat horns off a shelf and leave with them in her arms while Coyote slept. Witch Baby was very much in love. She had convinced Angel Juan to drive her up to Coyote's shack late at night and wait for her because, she said, Coyote had a present for them. Witch Baby was so in love that all she cared about was getting the horns. She didn't even think about how Coyote would feel when he woke a few moments after the red truck had disappeared down the hillside and saw that the familiar horn shadow was not falling across the floor in the moonlight.

When Witch Baby and Angel Juan got back

to Witch Baby's house, they sat in the dark truck.

"Well, aren't you going to let me see?" Angel Juan asked.

Witch Baby took the horns out from under her jacket and gave them to him.

"Oopa! Brujita!"

"They're for you. I asked Coyote if I could have them for you."

Angel Juan held the horns up on his head and looked at himself in the rearview mirror. His eyes shone, darker than the lenses of the sunglasses he almost always wore.

"Thank you, Baby. This is the coolest present. I feel like a real Goat Guy now."

Witch Baby looked down to hide the flowers blooming in her eyes, the heat in her cheeks. Angel Juan leaned over and kissed her face. Bristling roughness and shivery softness, heat and cool, honeysuckle and tobacco and fresh bread and spring. The horns gleaming like huge teeth in Angel Juan's lap. Then Witch Baby leaped out of the car.

"Wait! Baby!" Angel Juan leaned his head

out the window of the truck and watched her run into the shed. The horns were cool, pale bone.

Angel Juan attached them to a headband so he could wear them when he played bass. The next night, backstage at The Vamp, he put them on and admired himself in the mirror. He looked taller, his chin more angular, and he thought he noticed a shadow of stubble beginning to grow there. He took off his sunglasses and turned to Witch Baby.

"Hey, what do you think?"

"You are a fine-looking Goat Guy, Angel Juan."

Cherokee and Raphael came through the door. Raphael and Angel Juan hadn't been speaking since the fight, but now, wearing his horns, Angel Juan forgot all about it. And Raphael was so impressed by the horns that he forgot too.

"Cool horns," he said, swinging his tail.

Cherokee gasped and pulled Witch Baby aside.

"What did you do?" She dug her nails into Witch Baby's arm. "Coyote will kill us!"

"Let go, clutch! I did it because I love Angel Juan. Just like you got goat pants for your boyfriend."

"I didn't go against anyone's rules."

"You and your stupid clutchy rules!"

"We have to give them back! Witch!"

Witch Baby jammed her hand into her mouth and began gnawing on her nails. Cherokee looked over at Angel Juan. He was very handsome with his crown of horns and he was smiling.

Maybe it would be okay just this once, Cherokee thought. We could play one show with the horns. Angel Juan would feel so good. And maybe the horns are really magical. Maybe something magical will happen.

Angel Juan was still showing Raphael the horns. He looked over at Witch Baby. "That niña bruja got them for me. Pretty good job, hey?" He grinned.

Cherokee sighed. "Listen, Witch," she whispered. "We'll play one gig with the horns and then we'll tell Angel Juan that Coyote has to have them back. We'll get him another present. But we can't keep them."

Witch Baby didn't say anything. It was time to go on.

If the crowd had loved The Goat Guys before, had loved the Rasta boy with animal legs, the drummer witch with wings and the dancing blur of blonde and fringe and beads that was Cherokee, then tonight they loved the angel with horns.

Angel Juan's horns glowed above everything, pulsing with ivory light. His body moved as if he were the music he played. When he slid to his knees and lifted his bass high, the veins in his arms and hands were full.

We are a heart, Cherokee thought.

After the set, she watched Angel Juan pick Witch Baby up in his arms and swing her around. Cherokee had never seen either of them look so happy. She hated to think about taking the horns back to Coyote.

But Angel Juan has the confidence he needs now even without the horns, she told herself. We all do.

So at dawn the next morning, Cherokee untangled herself from Raphael, crawled out of the tepee and tiptoed across the wet lawn to the garden shed. She saw Witch Baby and Angel Juan lying together on the floor, their dark hair and limbs merged so that she could not tell them apart. Only when they moved slightly could she see both faces, but even then they wore the same dreamy smile, so it was hard to tell the difference. Then Cherokee saw the horns gleaming in a corner of the shed. She lifted them carefully, wrapped them in a sheet and carried them away with her.

Cherokee got on Raphael's bicycle and started to ride to Coyote's shack. But at the foot of Coyote's hill Cherokee stopped. She took the horns from the basket on the front of the bicycle and stroked them, feeling the weight, the smooth planes, the rough ridges, the sharp tips. She thought of last night onstage, the audience gazing up at The Goat Guys, hundreds of faces like frenzied lovers. It had never been like that before. She thought of the witch and angel twins, wrapped deep in the same dream on the floor of the garden shed.

Cherokee did not ride up the hill to Coyote's shack. Goat Guys, she whispered, turning the bike around. Beatles, Doors, Pistols, Goat Guys.

When Cherokee got home, the horns weighing heavy in the basket on the front of Raphael's bicycle, the sun had started to burn through the gray. Some flies were buzzing around the trash cans no one had remembered to take in.

Cherokee felt sweat pouring down the sides of her body and the sound of Raphael's guitar pounded in her head as she walked up the path.

Witch Baby was waiting in the living room eating Fig Newtons. She glared at Cherokee. "Where are they?"

Cherokee handed over the horns. Then she turned and went to her tepee, pulled the blanket over her head and fell asleep.

The wind blew a storm of feathers into her mouth, up her nostrils. Goats came trampling over the earth, stirring up clouds of dust. Horns of white flame sprang from their heads. And in the waves of a dark dream-sea floated chunks of bone, odd-shaped pieces with clefts in them like hooves.

At the next Goat Guy show, the band came on stage with their wings, their haunches, their horns. The audience swooned at their feet.

Cherokee spun and spun until she was dizzy, until she was not sure anymore if she or the stage was in motion.

Afterward two girls in lingerie and over-the-knee leather boots offered a joint to Raphael and Angel Juan. All four of them were smoking backstage when Cherokee and Witch Baby came through the door.

Witch Baby went and wriggled onto Angel Juan's lap. He was wearing the horns and massaging his temples. His face looked constricted with pain until he inhaled the smoke from the joint.

"Are you okay?" Witch Baby asked.

"My head's killing me."

Angel Juan offered the burning paper to Witch Baby. She inhaled, coughed and gave it to Raphael, who also took a hit.

"Want a hit, Kee?" he asked.

The girls in boots looked at each other, their lips curling back over their teeth.

"No thanks," Cherokee said. She went and stood next to Raphael and began playing with his hair.

The girls in boots crossed and uncrossed their legs, then stood up.

"We'll see you guys later," said one, looking straight at Raphael. The other smiled her snarl at Angel Juan. Then they left.

"Ick! Nasty!" Witch Baby hissed after them.

"I saw that one girl in some video at The Vamp," said Raphael. "She had cow's blood all over her. It was pretty sick." He took another hit from the joint and gave it back to Angel Juan.

"Let's get out of here," Cherokee said, wrinkling her nose at the burned smell in the air.

But the next time Raphael offered her a joint, she smoked it with him. The fire in her throat sent smoke signals to her brain in the shapes of birds and flowers. She leaned back against his chest and watched the windows glow.

"Square moons," she murmured. "New moons. Get it? New-shaped moon."

Later, in the dark kitchen, lit only by the luminous refrigerator frost, they ate chocolate chip ice cream out of the carton and each other's mouths.

But in the morning Cherokee's throat burned and her chest ached, dry. There were no more birds or flowers or window-moons, and when she tried to kiss Raphael he turned away from her.

The band played more and more shows. Cherokee's skull was full of music, even when it was quiet. Smoke made her chest heave when she tried to run. She remembered drinks and matches and eyes and mouths and breasts coming at her out of the darkness. She remembered brushing against Witch Baby's wings, feeling the stage shake as Raphael galloped across it; she remembered the shadow of horns on the wall behind them and Angel Juan massaging his temples. When she woke in the morning, she felt as if she had been dancing through her sleep, as if she had been awake in the minds of an audience whose dreams would not let her rest. And she did not want any of it to stop.

Some days, Angel Juan would drive Cherokee, Raphael and Witch Baby to school and then go to work. But more and more often they all just stayed home, piled in Weetzie's bed, watching soap operas and rented movies, eating tortilla chips and talking about ideas for new songs. At night they came to life, lighting up the house with red bulbs, listening to music, drinking beers, taking hot tubs on the deck by candlelight, dressing for the shows. At night they were vibrant—perfectly played instruments.

Sometimes Cherokee wanted to write to her family or visit Coyote, but she decided she was too tired, she would do it later, her head ached now. They would be out of school soon anyway, so what did it matter if they missed a few extra days, she told herself, running her hands over Raphael's thigh in the haunch pants. And they were doing something important. Lulu from The Vamp had told Raphael that she thought they could be the next hot new band.

Angel Juan and Witch Baby were kissing on the carpet. Through the open windows, the evening smelled like summer. It would be night soon. There would be feathers, fur and bone.

Omen

By daylight a fire fell. Three stars together it seemed: flaming, bearing tails. Out of the west it came, falling in a rain of sparks, running to east. The people saw, and screamed with a noise like the shaking of bells.

Aztec Indian

Dear Everybody,

I know the film is very important but sometimes I wish you were home. Maybe The Goat Guys can be in your next movie.

Love,
Cherokee

Hooves

Summer came and the canyon where Cherokee lived smelled of fires. Sometimes, when she stood on the roof looking over the trees and smog and listening to the sirens, she saw ash in the air like torn gray flesh. She wondered what Coyote was thinking as the hills burned around him. If lines had formed in his face when he had discovered that the horns were gone. Lines like scars. She had not spoken to him in weeks.

That summer there was dry fragile earth and burning weeds, buzzing electric wires, parched horns and the thought of Coyote's anger-scars. There was Cherokee's reflection in the mirror—powder-pale, her body narrow in the tight dresses she had started to wear. And there were the shows almost every night.

The shows were the only things that seemed to matter now. More and more people came, and when Cherokee whirled for them she forgot the heat that had kept her in a stupor all day, forgot the nightmares she had been having, the charred smell in the air and what Coyote was thinking. People were watching her, moving with her, hypnotized. And she was rippling and flashing above them. Onstage she was the fire.

And then one night, after a show, The Goat Guys came home and saw the package at the front door.

"It says 'For Cherokee.'"

Witch Baby handed over the tall box and Cherokee took it in her arms. At first she thought it was from her family. They were thinking of her. But then she saw the unfamiliar scrawl and she hesitated.

"Open it!" said Angel Juan.

"You have a fan, I guess," said Raphael.

Cherokee did not want to open the box. She sat staring at it.

"Go on!"

Finally, she tore at the tape with her nails, opened the flaps and removed the brown packing paper. Inside was another box. And inside that were the hooves.

They were boots, really. But the toes were curved, with clefts running down the front, and the platform heels were sharp wedges chiseled into the shape of animal hooves. They were made of something fibrous and tough. They looked almost too real.

"Now Cherokee will look like a Goat Guy too!" Angel Juan said.

"Totally cool!" Raphael picked up one of the boots. "I wish I had some like this!"

Cherokee sniffed. The hooves smelled like an animal. They bristled with tiny hairs.

"Put them on!"

She took off her moccasins and slid her feet into the boots. They made her tall; her legs were long like the legs of lean, muscled models who came to see The Goat Guys play. She walked around the room, balancing on the hooves.

"They are hot!" Raphael said, watching her.

They were fire. She was fire. She was thunderbird. Red hawk. Yellow dandelion. Storming the stage on long legs, on the feet of a horse child, wild deer, goat girl . . .

"Cherokee! Cherokee!"

They were calling her but she wasn't really listening. She was dancing, thrusting. Her voice was bells. Her tambourine sent off sparks. The Vamp audience reached for her, there at the bottom of the stage, there, beneath her hooves.

She spun and spun. She had imagined she was the color of red flame but she was whiter than ever, like the hottest part of the fire before it burns itself out.

Later, someone was reaching down her shirt. She called for Raphael but he was not there. Witch Baby came and pulled her away. Feathers were flying in a whirlwind. Her feet were blistering inside the hoof boots.

Then they were back at the house. Raphael had invited Lulu over and he, Lulu and Angel Juan were on the couch sharing a joint. Candles were burning. Raphael touched Lulu's smooth, dark cheek with the back of his hand. Or had Cherokee imagined that? Her feet hurt so much and in the candlelight she could have been mistaken.

"Help me take these off," she said to Witch Baby. "Please. They hurt."

Witch Baby pulled at one boot. Every part of her body strained, even the tendons in her neck. Finally she fell backward and Cherokee's foot was free, throbbing with pain. Witch Baby pulled on the other boot until it came off too.

"It cut me! Nasty thing!"

"What?"

"Your boot cut me." There was blood on

Witch Baby's hand.

"Let's wash it off."

They went into the bathroom and Cherokee held on to the claw-footed tub for balance. She felt as if she were going to be sick and took a deep breath. Then she helped clean the cut that ran across Witch Baby's palm like a red lifeline.

"I want to stop, Witch Baby," she whispered.

Witch Baby stood at the sink, her wings drooping with sweat and filth, her eyes glazed, blood from her hand dripping into the basin. "Tell that to our boyfriends out there on the couch," she said. "Tell that to Angel Juan's horns."

But what did Angel Juan's horns tell Angel Juan?

The next night The Goat Guys smoked and drank tequila before the show. Onstage they were all in a frenzy. Cherokee, burning with tequila, could not stop whirling, although her toes were screaming, smashed into the hooves. Witch Baby was playing so hard that the wings seemed to be flapping by themselves, ready to fly away with her. Raphael leaped up and down as if the fur pants were scalding him. Finally, he leaped into the audience and the people held him up, grabbing at matted fur, at his long dreadlocks, at his skin slippery with sweat.

While Raphael was thrashing around in the audience trying not to lose hold of his microphone, Angel Juan pumped his bass, charging forward with his whole body like a bull in a ring. He swung his head back and forth as if it were very heavy, crammed full of pain and sound. He slid to his knees. Something flashed in his hand. Cherokee thought she could hear the audience salivating as they yelled. They saw the knife before she did. They saw Angel Juan make the slash marks across his bare chest like a warrior painting himself before the fight. They reached out, hoping to feel his blood splash on them.

It was only surface cuts; The Goat Guys saw that later when they were at home cleaning him. But Cherokee's hands were trembling and her stomach felt as if she had eaten a live thing. She took the horns off Angel Juan's head.

He sat in a chair, his eyes half-closed.

Witch Baby was kneeling at his feet with a reddened washcloth in her hands. Raphael stood by himself, smoking a cigarette. They all watched Cherokee as she put the horns on the floor and backed away from them.

"We have to give them back to Coyote," she said.

"What are you talking about?"

"The horns. They don't belong to us. Coyote was here while we were out." Cherokee reached into her pocket and held out three glossy feathers she had found tied to the front door. "We have to give back the horns."

"You can't do that now," Witch Baby said. "Tomorrow night we'll have at least two record companies at our house! We need the horns!"

"Yeah, Cherokee, cool out," Angel Juan said. "You're just uptight about tomorrow."

"Look at you!" She pointed to his chest.

"He's all right. Lots of rock stars get carried away and do stuff like that. And we won't drink anything tomorrow," Raphael promised her.

She wanted him to hold her but lately they

almost never touched. After the shows they were always too exhausted to make love and collapsed together, chilled from their sweat and smelling of cigarettes, when they got back.

"And we're not even playing at a club. It'll be like my birthday party," Witch Baby said.

"Better! We're so much hotter now. Bob Marley, Jimi Hendrix, Jim Morrison, Elvis."

"I'm not doing any more shows 'til we give back the horns," Cherokee said. "Don't you see? We have to stop!"

"Don't worry," Raphael said. "Coyote gave us the horns. Why are you so afraid?"

Witch Baby began gnawing her cuticles, her eyes darting from Cherokee to Raphael. When Cherokee saw her, she just shook her head silently at Raphael. She couldn't tell him and Angel Juan the truth about the horns because she was afraid they wouldn't be able to forgive her and Witch Baby for what they had done.

When she fell asleep that night, Cherokee dreamed she was in a cage. It was littered with bones.

———

The night of the party, the house was crammed with people. They wore black leather and fur and drank tall, fluorescent-colored drinks. Some were in the bedrooms snorting piles of cocaine off mirrors. They were playing with the film equipment, pretending to surf on the surfboards, trying on beaded dresses and top hats, undressing the Barbie dolls and twisting the Mexican skeleton dolls' limbs together. There were some six-foot-tall models with bare breasts and necklaces made of teeth. Men with tattooed chests and scarred arms. The air was hot with bodies and smoke.

Before The Goat Guys played live, Raphael put on their tape—his own loping, reggae rap, Angel Juan's salsa-influenced bass, Witch Baby's rock-and-roll–slam drums, Cherokee's shimmery tambourine and backup vocals. A few people were dancing, doing the "goat." They rocked and hip-hopped in circles, butting each other with imaginary horns.

Cherokee was drinking from a bottle of whiskey someone had handed her when she saw Lulu go over to Raphael. Lulu was wearing a very short, low-cut black dress, and she leaned forward as she spoke to him. Cherokee could not hear what they were saying, but she saw Raphael staring down Lulu's dress, saw Lulu take his hand and lead him away. On the stereo, Raphael's voice was singing.

"White Dawn," Raphael sang. It was a song he had written when the band first started, a name he never used anymore.

Cherokee followed Raphael and Lulu into Weetzie's bedroom. She watched Lulu bend her head, as if she were admiring her reflection in a lake, and inhale the white powder off a mirror. She watched Raphael stand and flex his bare muscles. Lulu put her hands on Raphael's hips.

That was when Cherokee turned and ran out of the room.

First, she found Raphael's haunches lying in her closet. The hot, heavy fur scratched her arms when she lifted the pants. Next, she found Angel Juan's horns and Witch Baby's wings strewn on the floor of the living room among the bottles and cigarette butts, dolls, surf equipment and cannisters of film. Cherokee was already wearing the hooves.

She took the armload of fur and bone into the bathroom, pulled off her clothes, and stared at her reflection—a weak, pale girl, the shadows of her ribs showing bluish through her skin like an X ray.

I am getting whiter and whiter, she thought. Maybe I'll fade all the way.

But the hooves and haunches and horns and wings were not fragile. Everything about them was dark and full, even the fragrance that rose from them like the ghosts of the animals to whom they had once belonged. Cherokee had seen her friends transformed by these things, one at a time. She had seen Witch Baby soar, Raphael charge, Angel Juan glow. She had felt the wild pull of the hooves on her feet and legs. But what would it be like to wear all this power at once, Cherokee wondered. What creature could she become? What music would come from her, from her little white-girl body, when that body was something entirely different? How would they look at her then, all of them, those faces below her? How would Raphael look at her, how would his eyes shine, mirrors for her alone? He would look at her.

Cherokee stepped into the haunches. They made her legs feel heavy, dense with strength. Her feet in the boots stuck out from the bottom of the hairy pants as if both hooves and haunches were really part of her body. She fastened Witch Baby's wings to her shoulders and moved her shoulder blades together so that the wings stirred. Then she attached Angel Juan's horns to her head. In the mirror she saw a wild creature, a myth-beast, a sphinx. She shut her eyes, threw back her head and licked her lips.

I can do anything now, Cherokee thought, leaving the bathroom, passing among the people who had taken over the house so that she hardly recognized it anymore. Angel Juan was on the couch, surrounded by girls, their limbs flailing, but Cherokee didn't see Witch Baby anywhere.

Then Cherokee passed the room where Raphael and Lulu were sitting on the bed, staring at each other. Raphael did not take his eyes off Lulu as Cherokee walked by.

I don't need Raphael or Weetzie or Coyote or anybody, Cherokee told herself. She kept her eyes focused straight ahead of her and paraded like a runway model.

Cherokee climbed up the narrow staircase and out onto the roof deck, into the night. She could see the city below, shimmering beyond the dark canyon. Each of those lights was someone's window, each an eye that would see her someday and fill with desire and awe. Maybe tonight. Maybe tonight each of those people would gaze up at her, at this creature she had become, and applaud. And she wouldn't have to feel alone. Even without her family and Coyote. Even without the rest of The Goat Guys. Even without Raphael. She would fly above them on the wings she had made.

Cherokee swayed at the edge of the roof, gazing into the buoyant darkness. She felt the boots blistering her feet, the haunches scratching her legs, the horns pressing against her temples; but the wings, quivering with a slight breeze, would lift her away from all that, from anything that hurt. The way they had lifted Witch Baby from the mud.

Cherokee spread out her arms, poised.

And that was when she felt flight. But it was not the flight she had imagined.

Something had swept her away but it was not the wings carrying her into air. Something warm and steady and strong had swept her to itself. Something with a heartbeat and a scent of sage smoke. She was greeted, but not by an audience of anonymous lights, voices echoing her name. She recognized the voice that drew her close. It was Coyote's voice.

"Cherokee, my little one," Coyote wept. They were not the tears of silver—moons and stars—she had once imagined, but wet and salt as they fell from his eyes onto her face.

Dream Song

Where will you and I sleep?
At the down-turned jagged rim of the sky
you and I will sleep.

Wintu Indian

Dear Cherokee, Witch Baby, Raphael
and Angel Juan,

We are coming home.

Love,
Weetzie

Home

The first things Cherokee saw when she woke were the stained-glass roses and irises blossoming with sun. Then she shifted her head on the pillow and saw Raphael kneeling beside her.

"How are you feeling?" he whispered, his eyes on her face.

She nodded, trying to swallow as her throat swelled with tears.

"We're all going to take care of you."

"What about you?"

"Don't worry, Kee. Coyote said he is going to help all of us. I'm going to quit drinking and smoking, even. And he called Weetzie. They're all on their way home."

"What about Angel Juan's headaches?"

"Coyote is going to get some medicine together." He pressed his forehead to her chest, listening for her heart. "I'm so sorry, Cherokee."

"I just missed you so much."

"Me too. Where were we?"

Cherokee looked down at herself, small and white beneath the blankets. "Do you like me like this?" she asked. The tears in her throat had started to show in her eyes. "I mean, not all dressed up. I'm not like Lulu. . . ."

Raphael flung his arms around her and she saw the sobs shudder through his back as she stroked his head. "You are my beauty, White Dawn."

Coyote, Witch Baby and Angel Juan came

in with strawberries, cornmeal pancakes, maple syrup and bunches of real roses and irises that looked like the windows come to life. They gathered around the bed scanning Cherokee's face, the way Raphael had done, to see if she was all right.

"What happened?" Cherokee asked them.

"Witch Baby saw how you were acting at the party and she went to get Coyote," Angel Juan said, squinting and rubbing his temples.

"She told me all about the horns," Coyote said. "Forgive me, Cherokee."

"*I'm* sorry," Cherokee said. "About the horns."

"It's my fault!" said Witch Baby. "I should never have taken those clutch horns."

"Yes," said Coyote, "we were all at fault. But I am supposed to care for you and I failed."

"Did you know we had the horns?" Cherokee asked.

"I could have guessed. I turned my mind away from you. Sometimes, there on the hilltop, I forget life. Dreaming of past sorrows and the injured earth, I forget my friends and their children who are also my friends."

"What are we going to do?"

"I called your parents and they will be home in a few days."

"But will you help us now?" Cherokee asked. She looked over at Witch Baby, who was gazing at Angel Juan as if her head ached too. "Will you help take away Angel Juan's headaches and help Raphael stop smoking?"

The lines running through Coyote's face like scars were not from anger but concern. He took Cherokee's cold, damp hands in his own that were dry and warm, solid as desert rock. "I will help you," Coyote said.

After they had scrubbed the house clean, glued the broken bowls, washed the salsa- and liquor-stained tablecloths, waxed the scratched surfboards and fastened the dolls' limbs back on, Coyote, Cherokee, Raphael, Witch Baby and Angel Juan gathered in a circle on Coyote's hill.

Coyote lit candles and burned sage. In the center of the circle he put the tattered wings, haunches, horns and hooves. Then he began to chant and to beat a small drum with his flat, heavy palms.

"This is the healing circle," Coyote said. "First we will all say our names so that our ancestor spirits will come and join us."

"Angel Juan Perez."

"Witch Baby Wigg Bat."

"Raphael Chong Jah-Love."

"Cherokee Bat."

"Coyote Dream Song."

Coyote Dream Song chanted again. His voice filled the evening like the candlelight, like the smoke from the sage, like the beat of his heart.

"Now we will dance the sacred dances," Coyote said, and everyone stood, shyly at first, with their hands in their pockets or folded on their chests. Coyote jumped into the air as he played his drum, and the music moved in all of them until they were jumping too, leaping as high as they could. Then Coyote began to spin and they spun with him, circles making a circle, planets in orbit, everything becoming a blur of fragrant shadow and fragmented light around them.

"And we will dance our animal spirit," Coyote said, crouching, hunching his shoulders, his eyes flashing, his face becoming lean and secretive. The circle changed, then. There were ravens flying, deer prancing, obsidian elks dreaming.

Finally, the dancing ended and they sat, exhausted, leaning against each other, protected by ancestors who had recognized their names and glowing with the dream of the feathers and fur they might have been or would become.

"This is the healing circle," Coyote said. "So you may each say what it is you wish to heal. Or you may think it in silence." And he put his hand to his heart, then reached to the sky, then touched his heart again.

"The children in my country who beg in gutters and the hurt I gave to Witch Baby," Angel Juan said.

"My Angel Juan's headaches and all broken hearts," Witch Baby said.

"Cherokee's blistered feet and anything in the world that makes her sad," Raphael murmured.

"Our damaged earth. Angel Juan's headaches. Raphael's desire for smoke. Witch Baby's sweet heart. Cherokee's pain," Coyote said.

Wings, haunches, horns and hooves, thought Cherokee Bat. Wings, haunches, horns, hooves, home. Then, "All of you," she said aloud.

Coyote put his hand to his heart, reached to the sky, then touched his heart again.

That was when the wind came, a hot desert wind, a salt crystal wind, ragged with traveling, full of memories. It was wild like the wind that had brought Cherokee the feathers for Witch Baby's wings, but this time there were no feathers. This wind came empty, ready to take back. Cherokee imagined it extending cloud fingers toward them, toward the circle on the hill, imagined the crystalline gaze of the wind when it recognized Witch Baby's wings made from the feathers it had once brought.

The wings also recognized the wind and began to flap as if they were attached to a weak angel crouched in the center of the circle.

They flapped and flapped until they began to rise, staggering back and forth in the dust. Cherokee, Raphael, Witch Baby, Angel Juan and Coyote stared in silence as the wind reclaimed the wings and carried them off, flapping weakly into the evening sky.

Witch Baby stood and reached above her head, watching the wings disappear. Then she collapsed against Angel Juan and he held her.

"You don't need them," he whispered. "You make me feel like I have wings when you touch me." And as he spoke, one fragile feather, glinting with a streak of green, drifted down from the sky and landed upright in Witch Baby's hair.

Meanwhile, Raphael was inching toward the haunches that lay in front of him. Cherokee could see by his eyes that he wasn't sure if he was ready to give them up. But it was too late.

The goat had come down the hill. One old goat with white foamy fur and wet eyes. Unlike the goats who had come before, to give their fur to Coyote and Cherokee, this goat was quiet, so quiet that when he had gone, dragging the haunches in his mouth, Coyote and The Goat Guys were not sure if he had been there at all. Raphael started to stand, but Cherokee touched his wrist. He reached for her hand and they turned to see the goat being swallowed up by the hillside, a wave vanishing back into the ocean.

Cherokee knew what she had to do. Coyote was standing, facing her with a shovel in each hand. He held one out. Together, Cherokee and Coyote began to dig a hole in the dirt in the center of the circle. Dust clouds rose, glowing pink as the sun set, and the pink dust filled Cherokee's eyes and mouth.

The hooves were much heavier than they looked, heavier, even, than Cherokee remembered them, and the bristles poked out, grazing her bare arms. The hooves smelled bad, ancient, bitter. She dropped them into their grave. Then she and Coyote filled the grave up with earth and patted the earth with their palms. The dust settled, the sun slipped away, darkness eased over everything.

Coyote built a fire on the earth where the hooves were buried. The flames were dancers on a stage, swooning with their own beauty.

Angel Juan was staring into these flames. His horns lay at the edge of the fire and Cherokee remembered her dream of flame horns springing from goat foreheads. She watched Angel Juan stand and pick up the horns. Then Coyote held out his arms and Angel Juan went to him, placing the horns in Coyote's hands. Coyote set the horns down in the fire and embraced Angel Juan. Like a little boy who has not seen his father in many years, Angel Juan buried his head against Coyote's chest. All the pride and strength in his slim shoulders seemed to fall away as Coyote held him. When he moved back to sit beside Witch Baby, his forehead was smooth, no longer strained with the weight or the memory of the horns.

Later, after Cherokee, Raphael, Witch Baby and Angel Juan had left, looking like children who have played all day in the sea and eaten sandy fruit in the sun and gone home sleepy and warm and safe; later, when the fire had gone out, Coyote took the horns from the log ashes and brushed them off. Then Coyote

Dream Song carried the horns back inside.

When Cherokee and Raphael got back to the canyon house, they set up the tepee on the grass and crept inside it. They lay on their backs, not touching, looking at the leaf shadows flickering on the canvas, and trying to identify the flowers they smelled in the warm air.

"Honeysuckle."

"Orange blossom."

"Rose."

"The sea."

"The sea! That doesn't count!"

"I smell it like it's growing in the yard."

They giggled the way they used to when they were very young. Then they were quiet. Raphael sat up and took Cherokee's feet in his hands.

"Do they still hurt?" he asked, stroking them tenderly. He moved his hands up over her whole body, as if he were painting her, bringing color into her white skin. As if he were playing her—his guitar. And all the hurt seemed to float out of her like music.

They woke in the morning curled together.

"Remember how when we were really little we used to have the same dreams?" Cherokee whispered.

"It was like going on trips together."

"It stopped when we started making love."

"I know."

"But last night . . ."

"Orchards of hawks and apricots," Raphael said, remembering.

"Sheer pink-and-gold cliffs."

"The sky was wings."

"The night beasts run beside us, not afraid. Dream-horses carry us . . ."

"To the sea," they said together as they heard a car pull into the driveway and their parents' voices calling their names.

At the end of the summer, The Goat Guys set up their instruments on the redwood stage their families had helped them build behind the canyon house. Thick sticks of incense burned and paper lanterns shone in the trees like huge white cocoons full of electric butterflies. A picnic of salsa, home-baked bread still steaming in its crust, hibiscus lemonade and cake decorated with fresh flowers was spread on the lawn. Summer had ripened to its fullest—a fruit ready to drop, leaving the autumn tree glowing faint amber with its memory as the band played on the stage for their families and friends.

Cherokee looked at the rest of The Goat Guys playing their instruments beside her. Even dressed in jeans and T-shirts, Raphael and Angel Juan could pout and gallop and butt the air. Witch Baby seemed to hover, gossamer, above her seat. The music moved like a running creature, like a creature of flight, and Cherokee followed it with her mind. She was a pale, thin girl without any outer layers of fur or bone or feathers to protect or carry her. But she could dance and sing, there, on the stage. She could send her rhythms into the canyon.